National REGULAR Average ORDINARY Day

by Lisa Katzenberger

illustrated by Barbara Bakos

Penguin Workshop

Peter did not like being bored. It was the complete and total, absolute worst!

Hanging out with his neighbor Devin was usually pretty fun. But lately it seemed like they'd been playing the same games over and over.

Action figures.

Shooting hoops.

Building blocks.

Action figures.

Shooting hoops.

Building blocks.

Action figures.

Shooting hoops.

Building blocks.

"Enough!" Peter yelled.

He stomped off toward home, where he sighed . . .
and pouted . . . and twiddled his thumbs. It was awful.

So Peter created a plan to make sure there would always
be exciting new ways to have fun.
He would find a different holiday to celebrate each day!

Peter even rated each holiday on a scale of 1 to 10 stars.
A 10 was the best!

★★★★★
★★★★

There was National
Ice-Cream Sandwich Day
(9 stars).

★★★★

National Bow Tie Day (4 stars)

Even National Underwear Day (an unexpected 8 stars).

But one morning, Peter woke up to a disappointing discovery. There was NO HOLIDAY!

No National Tell a Joke Day (9 stars). No National Waffle Day (7 stars).
ot even National Lighthouse Day (2 stars)!
Nothing to celebrate? How would he know what to do for fun?

But if there was one thing Peter had learned, it was that *anything* could be a holiday. All he had to do was make one up!

First, he attempted National Ride Your Bike with No Hands Day (3 stars).

Next, he gave National Walking Backward Day a shot (2 stars).

He even tried National Ignore Your Sister Day (1 star).

Peter needed to think bigger. Maybe he could combine some of the holidays into one.

But celebrating both National Squirrel Appreciation Day and National Bubble Bath Day was a bit of a challenge (1 star).

A mash-up of National Eat What You Want Day and
National Dance Day *seemed* like a good idea . . .

But not so much (0 stars).

Peter was still bored, bored, BORED!

He figured he might as well just sit in a box and wait for the day to end.

He sighed . . .

And pouted . . .

And twiddled his thumbs . . .

And then . . .

Peter realized he wasn't in a box at all. It was a race car, dashing down a speedway! It was a rocket, zooming toward Mars! It was a ship, cruising the rumbling seas!

Just then, Devin rode by. "What are you doing?"
Peter shrugged. "Just pretending."
"Another holiday, huh?" Devin said.
"Not this time. They got to be kind of exhausting."
Peter watched Devin do tricks on his bike. It looked pretty cool.

"Sorry about how I acted the other day," Peter said.
"Do you want to play?"

As Peter and Devin played regular, average, ordinary games, other kids joined in.

Soon, Peter's block was bursting with activity. And instead of being bored, he was buzzing with energy.

Peter didn't need something special to do every single day to stay entertained. An ordinary day could be fun, too.

He even gave it a name: National Regular Average Ordinary Day.

And *that* was something to celebrate.